The KnowHow Book of Fishing

Anne Civardi and Fred Rashbrook

Illustrated by Colin King
Designed by John Jamieson

Contents

Usborne Publishing

Special fish illustrations on pages 1, 20, 21, 22, 23, 28 and 29 by George Thompson

Editorial Consultant: Angela Littler

First Published in 1976
Usborne Publishing Ltd
20 Garrick Street
London WC2E 9BJ

© Usborne Publishing Ltd 1976

Printed in Great Britain by: Purnell & Sons Ltd. Paulton (Avon) and London.

About This Book

This book shows you how to fish from land with bait, the cheapest and easiest kind of fishing to do.

It tells you about two sorts of bait-fishing; freshwater fishing–in ponds, lakes, rivers and streams–and saltwater fishing–in estuaries and from the seashore.

This book does not tell you about more complicated and expensive kinds of fishing, such as fly fishing, spinning and fishing from boats.

It shows you how to put floats, weights, hooks and bait on the fishing line, and the kinds of bait to use to catch different sorts of fish.

It also shows you where the fish live and feed, and where you are likely to catch them.

On page 4 we show you how to make a rod yourself. As there are lots of rods and reels you can buy, we have suggested the kinds that will be easiest to use. If you are not sure what sort to choose, ask for help in a fishing tackle shop.

Anglers use lots of special words about fishing. We have tried to explain them in the book, but if you come across one you don't understand, the list on page 32 may help you.

Kinds of Fishing

Freshwater Fishing

There are two sorts of fishing you can do in freshwater. They are called float fishing and leger fishing.

1 Float Fishing

THIS IS WHEN YOU USE A FLOAT AND LITTLE WEIGHTS, CALLED SPLIT SHOT, TO FISH WITH. THE WATER SHOULD NOT BE VERY DEEP AND YOU SHOULD FISH CLOSE INTO THE BANK.

2 Leger Fishing

THIS IS WHEN YOU USE WEIGHTS BUT NO FLOAT ON THE LINE. THE WATER CAN BE DEEP, THE CURRENT STRONG AND YOU CAN CAST FAR OUT INTO THE WATER.

Seashore Fishing

There are two sorts of fishing you can do from the seashore. They are called sea float fishing and sea leger fishing.

1 Sea Float Fishing

THIS IS WHEN YOU USE A FLOAT AND A SMALL WEIGHT ON THE LINE. THE WATER SHOULD BE CALM AND YOU FISH CLOSE INTO THE SHORE.

2 Sea Leger Fishing

THIS IS WHEN YOU USE A HEAVY WEIGHT AND NO FLOAT ON THE LINE. THEN YOU CAN FISH FAR OUT INTO THE WATER AND WHERE THE CURRENT IS STRONG.

The Things an Angler Uses

Anglers use lots of different kinds of fishing equipment.
You can make some of it yourself, such as freshwater floats,
landing nets and even a simple rod. The rest you can buy
quite cheaply from any fishing tackle shop.

Rods

Your rod will probably
be made of fibre-glass
with a cork handle and
metal reel fittings.
Your line is wound on
to a reel which fits
into the reel fittings.

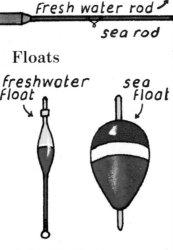

Fresh water rod

sea rod

Reels

fixed spool reel

There are lots of
reels you can buy.
This is one of the
best and easiest
kinds to use.

Fishing Line

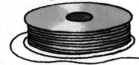

The best kind to use
is monofilament line.
Buy it in 100 m spools.
For freshwater, the
breaking strain should
be about 2 kg. For sea
fishing, about 8 kg.

Hooks

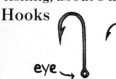

eye

Buy the hooks with
eyes. They are the
easiest kind to tie
to fishing line.

Hook Lengths

Anglers often keep
their hooks tied to
short pieces of nylon
line. These are called
hook lengths. They are
finer than the fishing
line which makes them
hard for fish to see.

Floats

freshwater
float

sea
float

A float is fixed to
the fishing line. It
keeps the hook at the
right depth and shows
you when a fish bites.
It is painted brightly
on top so you can see
it in the water. The
part that goes under
the water is dark so
fish cannot see it.

Float Rings

float rings

These are rubber rings
which are used to fix
floats to fishing line.

Baits

These are bits of food,
such as bread, cheese,
maggots, garden worms,
lugworms, prawns and
mussels. You put them
on to the hook to
catch different kinds
of fish.

Weights

Anglers fit different
kinds of lead weights
to the fishing line
above the hook. In
float fishing, the
weights keep the bait
down and the float
upright. In leger
fishing, they keep the
bait on the bottom.

Split shot are little
balls of lead with a
slit in them which are
used as weights in
freshwater float
fishing.

Sea float weights are
bigger and heavier
than split shot. They
keep a sea float
upright in the water
and the bait hanging
at the right depth.

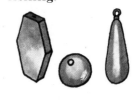

Freshwater leger
weights are heavier
and bigger than split
shot and are used
without floats.

Sea leger weights are
heavy weights used in
sea fishing. The
heavier they are, the
further out you can
cast the line.

Swivels

Swivels are small
metal things which
allow the hook and
weights to turn round
and round without
twisting the line.

Landing Nets

Most anglers take a
net with them when
they go fishing to help
them land big fish.

Rods and Reels

If you want a really simple and cheap rod, make the home-made one on this page. You will be able to catch little fish in shallow water with it.

To catch bigger fish you will need to buy a proper rod and reel from a fishing tackle shop. Ask the tackle dealer to help you choose the right rod.

The best kind of reel to use is the fixed spool reel. It has a metal arm which goes round and round to wind the fishing line on to a fixed spool.

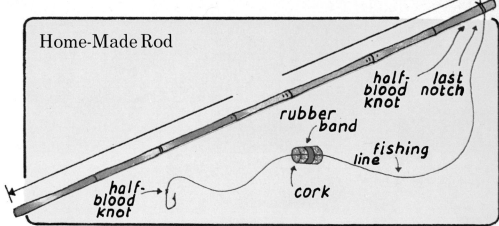

Home-Made Rod

Buy a bamboo cane, about 3 metres long, from a garden shop. Tie some nylon fishing line, just over 3 metres long, below the top notch, like this.

Wind a rubber band round a cork. Fix the cork about half-way up the line, as shown, to use as a float. Then tie a hook to the end of the line.

Fixed Spool Reel

This is an easy reel to fish with once you learn how to use it properly. You need a stronger and bigger one for sea fishing than for freshwater fishing.

When you turn the reel handle the metal arm, called the bale arm, spins round and round, winding the fishing line on to a fixed spool.

When you open the bale arm, the reel line can run off the spool. As soon as you turn the reel handle, the arm clicks shut automatically and stops the line running off the spool.

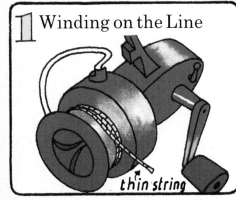

1 Winding on the Line

Fix the reel on to the rod handle and open the bale arm. Then wind some thin string round the reel spool until it is about half full.

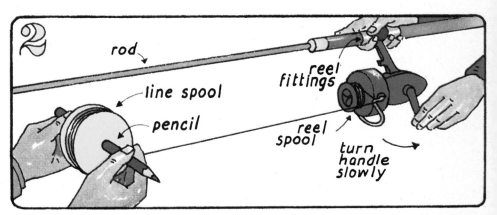

2

Tie the fishing line to the end of the string. Put a pencil through the line spool and ask a friend to hold it. Now turn the reel handle slowly to wind the line on to the reel.

Keep the line tight as you wind it on to the reel. The reel must not have too much line on it. Cut the line when it is about 3 mm from the rim of the reel.

4

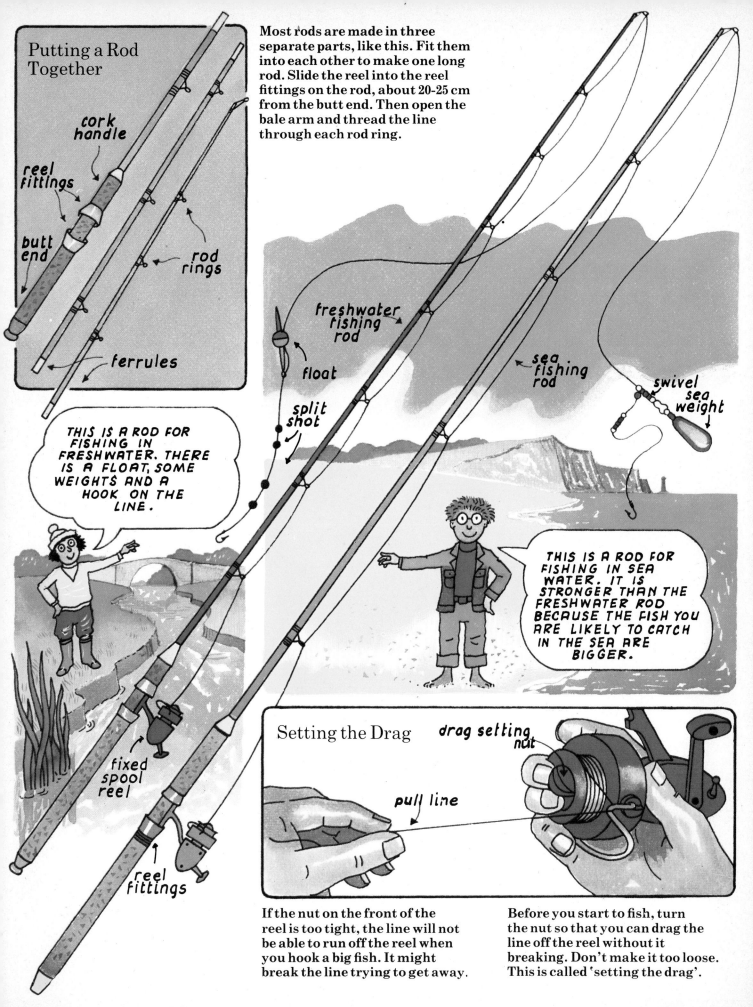

Putting a Rod Together

cork handle

reel fittings

butt end

rod rings

ferrules

Most rods are made in three separate parts, like this. Fit them into each other to make one long rod. Slide the reel into the reel fittings on the rod, about 20-25 cm from the butt end. Then open the bale arm and thread the line through each rod ring.

freshwater fishing rod

float

split shot

sea fishing rod

swivel

sea weight

THIS IS A ROD FOR FISHING IN FRESHWATER. THERE IS A FLOAT, SOME WEIGHTS AND A HOOK ON THE LINE.

THIS IS A ROD FOR FISHING IN SEA WATER. IT IS STRONGER THAN THE FRESHWATER ROD BECAUSE THE FISH YOU ARE LIKELY TO CATCH IN THE SEA ARE BIGGER.

fixed spool reel

reel fittings

Setting the Drag

drag setting nut

pull line

If the nut on the front of the reel is too tight, the line will not be able to run off the reel when you hook a big fish. It might break the line trying to get away.

Before you start to fish, turn the nut so that you can drag the line off the reel without it breaking. Don't make it too loose. This is called 'setting the drag'.

Knots and Hints

These are the special knots you need to know for fishing. If you use ordinary knots they will slip on nylon line and you will lose some of your tackle.

Practise tying them so that you can put all the tackle in this book together very quickly.

We have used different coloured line to make it easier for you to see how to tie them.

Simple Loop Knot

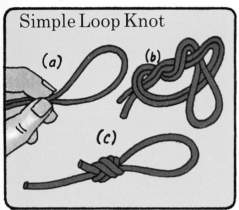

(a) (b)

(c)

Use this kind of knot to make a strong loop at the end of the reel line or a hook length.

Double Loop Knot

(a) simple loop (b)

simple loop

Join hook lengths to the end of the reel line with a double loop knot.

Stop Knot

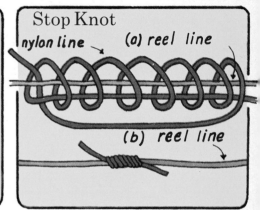

nylon line (a) reel line

(b) reel line

When you use a sliding float, tie a stop knot on to the fishing line above the float.

Half-Blood Knot

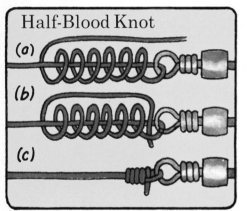

(a)

(b)

(c)

Tie quick-release swivels, barrel swivels and hooks with eyes to the line with a half-blood knot.

Blood Knot

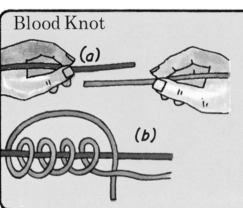

(a)

(b)

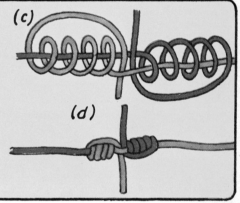

(c)

(d)

Use this knot to join two lengths of nylon fishing line together.

You can also use it to tie the fishing line to the string you wind on to the fixed spool reel.

Blood Loop

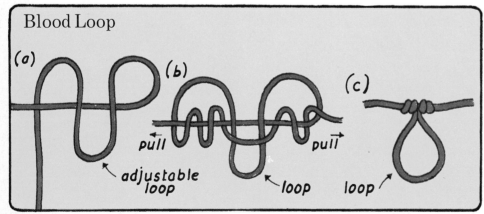

(a)

(b)

(c)

pull

pull

adjustable loop

loop

loop

This is how you make a blood loop in a paternoster line for seashore fishing. It is difficult to tie and needs lots of practice.

The loops should be big enough to stick out from the line and to put a hook on.

Hook Lengths

hook length line (finer than reel line)

simple loop

half-blood knot

Make up some hook lengths with different size hooks. Tie one to the reel line instead of a hook. It is much quicker. Line often gets broken or tangled and you have to change hooks quickly.

Holding Fish

wet cloth

Most of the freshwater fish you catch have to be put back in the water. Always wet your hands before you hold a fish, or use a wet rag. It stops you from rubbing off the fish's scales and hurting it.

1 Unhooking – By Hand

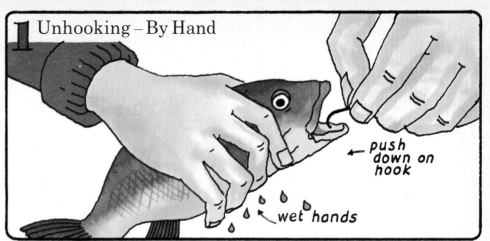

push down on hook

wet hands

Try very hard not to hurt fish you are going to put back in the water. If the hook is in the lip or on the edge of the fish's mouth, take it out with your fingers.

Push down very gently on the hook to free the end or the barb. Then slide it out of the fish's mouth. When you unhook a big fish, lie it on some wet grass or in a wet landing net.

2 Unhooking – With a Disgorger

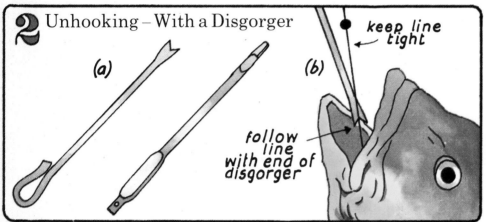

(a)

keep line tight

(b)

follow line with end of disgorger

If the hook is right down the fish's throat, use a disgorger to get it out. These two kinds (a) are the best ones to use. Buy them from a tackle shop.

Slide the disgorger down the fishing line. Then slip it on to the bend of the hook and press down gently to free the barb from the fish's throat (b).

Keeping Records

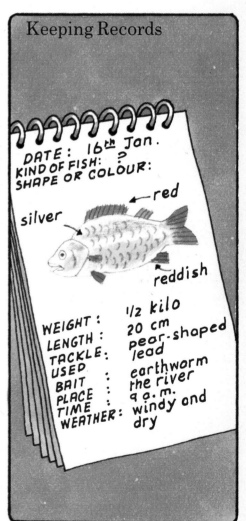

DATE: 16th Jan.
KIND OF FISH: ?
SHAPE OR COLOUR:

silver

red

reddish

WEIGHT: ½ kilo
LENGTH: 20 cm
TACKLE: pear-shaped lead
USED
BAIT: earthworm
PLACE: the river
TIME: 9 a.m.
WEATHER: windy and dry

It is a good idea to keep a log book of the fish you catch. Write down the important things, such as the name, weight and length of the fish, the tackle and bait you used and the time of day. Then you will have a record of the best ways to catch different fish.

Weighing Your Catch

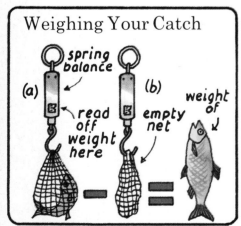

spring balance

(a)

read off weight here

(b)

empty net

weight of

Put the fish into a wet net. Hook the net on to a spring balance, like this. Read off the weight (a). Subtract the weight of the net afterwards to get the weight of the fish only (b).

Looking After Tackle

Keep your rod in a bag and your reel in a box between fishing trips. After fishing, clean off any dirt or sand. Oil all the ferrules.

Hooks must always be very sharp. Sharpen the points with a sharpening stone or sandpaper. Dry the hooks before you put them away to stop them rusting. After fishing, cut any frayed or worn bits off the reel line.

Fishing Gear

You can save money and have a lot of fun making bits of fishing gear yourself.

These two pages show you how to make some things you will find useful. They also show you what weights and hooks to buy for freshwater fishing.

You will need
For the Landing Net
2 wire coat hangers
a strong wooden stick (about 1.5 metres long)
a big net vegetable bag (ask for one at a vegetable shop)
string and waterproof tape
a hair grip or a big darning needle
For the Float Box
a plastic box with a lid
strong elastic thread
sheet sponge, waterproof glue and scissors
For the Rod Rest
a wire coat hanger and string
a strong stick and a penknife
For the Hook Box
a plastic box with a lid
sheet sponge and a cork
waterproof glue and scissors

1 Landing Net

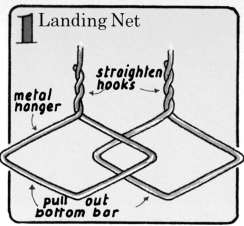

Straighten out the hooks on two metal coat hangers. Then pull out the bottom bars so that both hangers are a diamond shape.

2

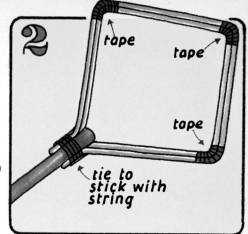

Tape the two hangers together, like this. Then tie them to the end of the strong stick with string. Use lots of string and make sure it is very tight.

1 Float Box

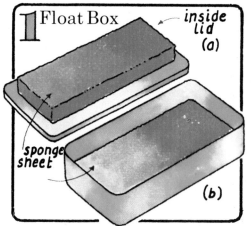

Glue a piece of sheet sponge to the inside of the box lid, about 2 cm from each side (a). Glue sheet sponge to the bottom of the box as well (b).

2

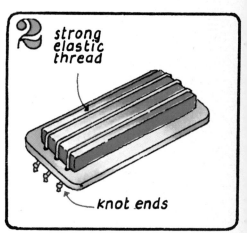

Make three holes with scissors in each end of the lid. Thread a bit of elastic through each pair of holes, like this. Tie knots in the ends.

1 Rod Rest

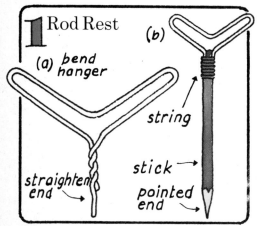

Straighten the hook on a wire coat hanger. Bend the hanger to this shape (a). Trim one end of a stick to a point. Tie the hanger to the other end with string (b).

2

Always take a rod rest with you when you go fishing. You need two for leger fishing. Put your rod on them, like this, while you are waiting for a fish to bite.

3

Hold the rod yourself when you use a float. Only leave it on the rod rest when you put bait on the hook, hold or land a fish. Never lie your rod on the ground.

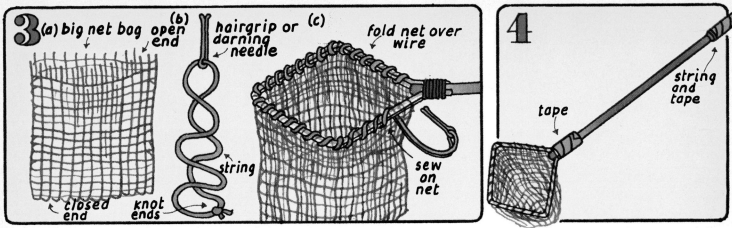

3 (a) big net bag open end (b) hairgrip or darning needle (c) fold net over wire

string

closed end   knot ends   sew on net

Cut off the top of the big net vegetable bag until it is about 35 cm deep (a). Thread string through a hair grip or a big darning needle. Knot the ends (b).

Fold the open end of the net bag over the wire frame. Sew it to the frame with the string, going over and over (c). If the net is too big, gather the edge together as you sew.

4   tape   string and tape

Wind string round the bottom of the stick for a handle. Cover it with waterproof tape. Then cover the string at the other end of the stick with waterproof tape.

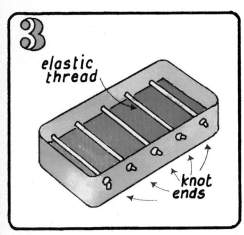

3   elastic thread   knot ends

Make five holes in opposite sides of the plastic box, as shown. Thread a bit of strong elastic through each pair of holes. Tie knots in the ends.

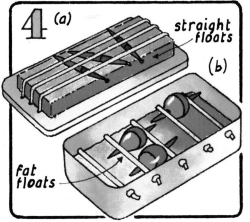

4 (a)   straight floats   (b)   fat floats

Keep your straight floats under the elastic thread on the box lid (a). Keep fat ones and long ones under the elastic on the bottom of the box (b).

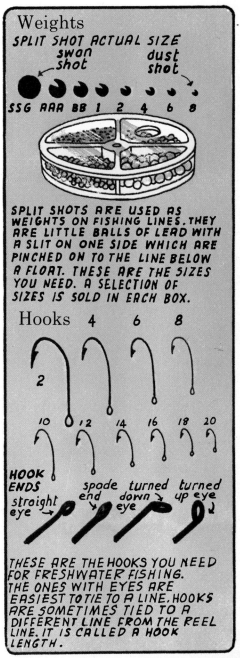

Weights

SPLIT SHOT ACTUAL SIZE

swan shot   dust shot

SSG AAA BB 1 2 4 6 8

SPLIT SHOTS ARE USED AS WEIGHTS ON FISHING LINES. THEY ARE LITTLE BALLS OF LEAD WITH A SLIT ON ONE SIDE WHICH ARE PINCHED ON TO THE LINE BELOW A FLOAT. THESE ARE THE SIZES YOU NEED. A SELECTION OF SIZES IS SOLD IN EACH BOX.

Hooks   4   6   8

2

10   12   14   16   18   20

HOOK ENDS   spade end   turned down eye   turned up eye
straight eye

THESE ARE THE HOOKS YOU NEED FOR FRESHWATER FISHING. THE ONES WITH EYES ARE EASIEST TO TIE TO A LINE. HOOKS ARE SOMETIMES TIED TO A DIFFERENT LINE FROM THE REEL LINE. IT IS CALLED A HOOK LENGTH.

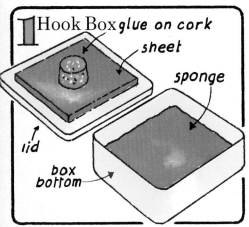

1 Hook Box glue on cork sheet   sponge

lid   box bottom

Glue a piece of sheet sponge to the inside of the box lid. Glue some to the bottom of the box too. Then glue a cork to the middle of the lid, like this.

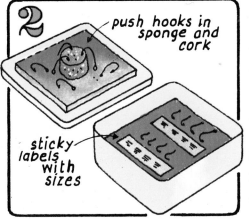

2   push hooks in sponge and cork   sticky labels with sizes

Push your hooks into the sponge and cork to keep them sharp and safe. Group them in size order. Stick labels with the size numbers above each group.

Making Freshwater Floats

These are some freshwater floats you can make. The longer they are, the more weights they need on the line below them to float upright in the water. Sea fishing floats are bigger and difficult to make. It is better to buy them.

Always glue up the ends of the float to seal them and make them water-tight. Let the glue dry before you paint the float.

You will need
2 big feathers (chicken, duck or turkey feathers will do)
a cork
a plastic drinking straw
a thin, wooden stick or thin dowel (about 15 cm long and as thick as a pencil)
2 wooden golf tees
a peacock quill from a tackle shop
a ping pong ball
fine sandpaper, a penknife and waterproof glue (Copydex)
thin wire and some thread
rubber float rings from a tackle shop (to fix the float to the fishing line)
scissors and a paint brush
waterproof paint (craft paints or special float paints)

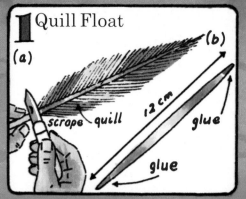

1 Quill Float

Starting from the thick end of the feather, scrape clean about 12 cm (a). Cut it off – this is the quill. Cut the thin end until it is as thin as a match. Glue up both ends (b).

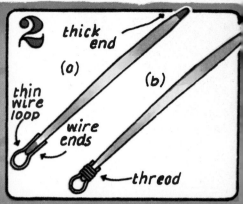

2

Rub the quill with sandpaper. Loop a bit of wire round the thin end (a). Wind thread round the wire ends and coat it with glue (b). This is called whipping.

3

Paint 3 cm of the thick end of the quill a bright colour. Paint the rest a dark colour. Leave it to dry. Then slide a rubber float ring on to the thick end.

1 Quill and Cork Float

Make a hole through the middle of a cork with thin scissors or a knitting needle. Do not make the hole too big. The cork is for the body of the float.

2

Shape the cork with a sharp knife until it is about this size (a). Then smooth off the rough corners with fine sandpaper (b).

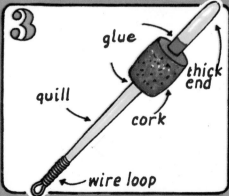

3

Clean off, trim, sandpaper and glue a quill as in Quill Float 1 above. Push the quill through the hole in the cork. Glue up the holes. Then whip on a wire loop.

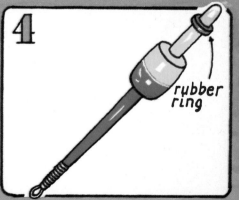

4

Paint the thick end and half the cork a bright colour. Paint the rest a dark, murky colour. Leave the float to dry. Then slide on a rubber float ring.

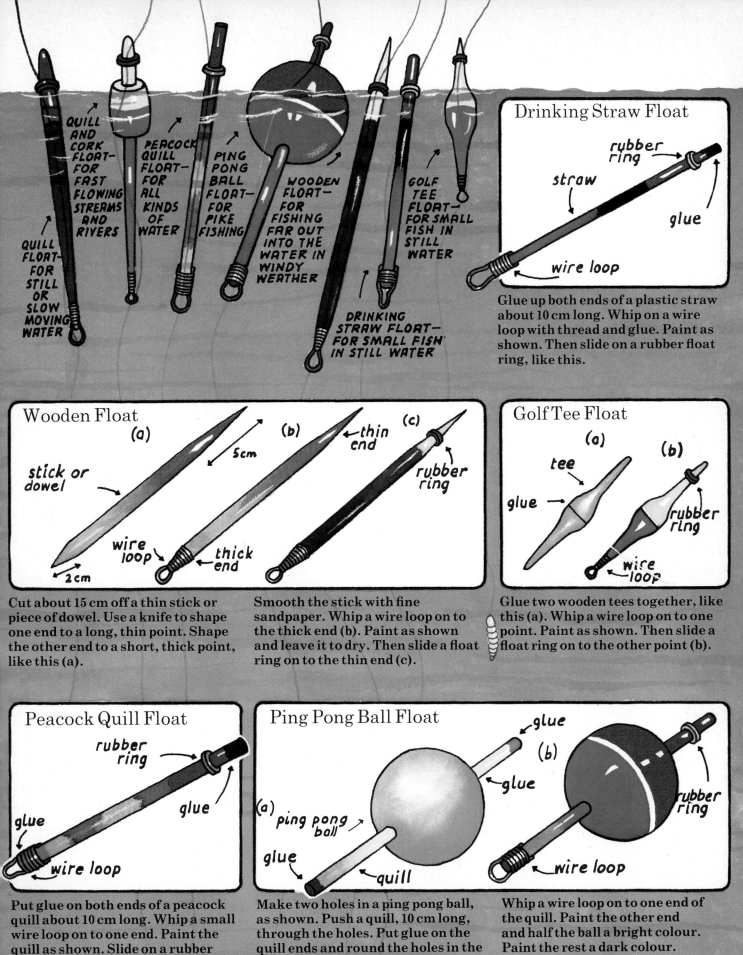

QUILL AND CORK FLOAT—FOR FAST FLOWING STREAMS AND RIVERS

PEACOCK QUILL FLOAT—FOR ALL KINDS OF WATER

PING PONG BALL FLOAT—FOR PIKE FISHING

WOODEN FLOAT—FOR FISHING FAR OUT INTO THE WATER IN WINDY WEATHER

GOLF TEE FLOAT—FOR SMALL FISH IN STILL WATER

QUILL FLOAT—FOR STILL OR SLOW MOVING WATER

DRINKING STRAW FLOAT—FOR SMALL FISH IN STILL WATER

Drinking Straw Float

Glue up both ends of a plastic straw about 10 cm long. Whip on a wire loop with thread and glue. Paint as shown. Then slide on a rubber float ring, like this.

Wooden Float

Cut about 15 cm off a thin stick or piece of dowel. Use a knife to shape one end to a long, thin point. Shape the other end to a short, thick point, like this (a).

Smooth the stick with fine sandpaper. Whip a wire loop on to the thick end (b). Paint as shown and leave it to dry. Then slide a float ring on to the thin end (c).

Golf Tee Float

Glue two wooden tees together, like this (a). Whip a wire loop on to one point. Paint as shown. Then slide a float ring on to the other point (b).

Peacock Quill Float

Put glue on both ends of a peacock quill about 10 cm long. Whip a small wire loop on to one end. Paint the quill as shown. Slide on a rubber float ring.

Ping Pong Ball Float

Make two holes in a ping pong ball, as shown. Push a quill, 10 cm long, through the holes. Put glue on the quill ends and round the holes in the ping pong ball (a).

Whip a wire loop on to one end of the quill. Paint the other end and half the ball a bright colour. Paint the rest a dark colour. Slide on a float ring (b).

Casting and Landing

Swinging the rod to drop the hook into the water at the right spot is called casting. It takes lots of practice. Practise in a field or garden with a small weight on the line and no hook.

The hardest part is letting go of the line at the right moment. When you get very good you will be able to get the hook and bait to the right spot every time.

As soon as a fish bites, reel in slowly and land it. If you don't get a bite after a few minutes when you are float fishing, reel in the line and cast again.

1 Underarm Cast

Hold the rod handle in your right hand. Open the bale arm of the reel and press the line against the rod with your first finger. Then hold the line in your left hand, just above the hook, as shown.

2

Gently swing out the line, lifting up your finger at the end of the swing. As soon as the hook-bait hits the water, turn the reel handle to close the bale arm.

3

Wind the handle until the fishing line is tight right down to the float. Use this underarm cast when you are fishing with floats.

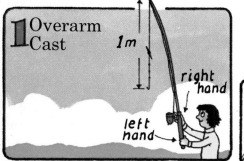

1 Overarm Cast

1m
right hand
left hand

Use an overarm cast when your fishing spot is far out from the bank. Pull one metre of line below the rod tip. Hold the rod up with both hands, like this.

2

swing line clear

Open the bale arm and press the line against the rod with your finger. Swing the rod back a bit. Aim at the right spot in the water and jerk the rod forwards.

3

jerk rod forwards

When your right arm is straight, lift up your first finger to let the line fly out. As soon as it hits the water, close the bale arm and wind the reel handle to tighten up the line.

1 Beach Casting

1m
weight
feet apart

Pull about one metre of line from the rod tip to the weight. Stand with your feet apart and your left shoulder towards the direction you are going to cast.

2 right hand   left hand

Hold the rod in both hands. Open the bale arm. Press your finger against the line. Swing the rod right back. Jerk it forwards, pulling down with your left hand and pushing forwards with your right.

3

When your right arm is straight, lift up your finger and let the line fly out. When the weight has sunk to the bottom, close the bale arm and tighten the line.

Hand Landing

If you catch a little fish, you don't need a net to land it in. Just swing it straight into your hand. Hold its head and shoulders gently so that you don't hurt it.

1 Net Landing

rod tip bent

keep line tight

When you catch a big fish, use your landing net. Hold the rod upright so that the fish pulls against the rod tip. Keep the line very tight or the fish might wriggle off the hook.

2

rod tip straight

The rod tip will straighten out when the fish gets tired. Now reel in very slowly, keeping the fish just under the water. Slide the landing net under it when you get it to the bank.

1 Beach Landing

If you hook a big fish from the beach reel it in very slowly until it is partly out of the water. Then walk backwards up the beach and wait for a big wave.

2

Let the wave wash the fish safely up the shingle or sand where you can pick it up. Never try to lift it out of the water on the end of your line. You might break the line and lose the fish.

IMPORTANT!

WATCH OUT FOR TREES AND BUSHES BEHIND YOU AS YOU CAST. YOUR LINE MIGHT GET TANGLED UP IN THEM.

TRY NOT TO MAKE SHADOWS ON THE WATER. THEY SCARE THE FISH AWAY. STAND WITH THE SUN SHINING TOWARDS YOU IF POSSIBLE.

DON'T JUMP ABOUT ON THE BANK OR MAKE TOO MUCH NOISE. FISH CAN HEAR VERY WELL AND WILL SWIM OFF AT THE SLIGHTEST SOUND.

NEVER REEL IN A FISH ON TOP OF THE WATER. IT WILL THRASH ABOUT AND FRIGHTEN OFF THE FISH NEARBY.

Freshwater Baits

Most freshwater fish will eat different sorts of bait. If you don't catch any fish with one kind, try another. Baits put on hooks are called hook-baits.

Keep bread and cheese baits in a wet cloth to stop them from crumbling. Put worms in an old box with damp garden soil, vegetable scraps and tea leaves.

You are much more likely to catch a fish if you use ground-bait. This is bait you put into the water near the fishing spot.

Bread Baits

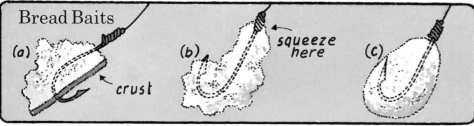

(a) crust (b) squeeze here (c)

Nearly all freshwater fish like bread baits. Put a small bit of crust on the hook, like this (a) or press some fresh bread round the bend of the hook, like this (b).

Use lumps of bread paste. Make it by wetting some stale bread. Put it in a rag and squeeze out the water. Shape it into lumps (c). Use hook sizes 8-14 for bread baits.

Cheese Baits

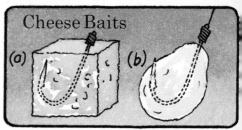

(a) (b)

Cheese is a good bait for chub. Use any fairly soft cheese, either in small cubes (a) or mixed with bread paste (b). Use hook sizes 6-8 for cheese baits.

1 Minnows

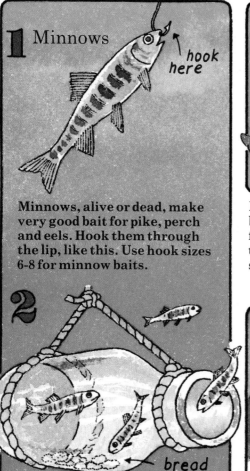

hook here

bread

Minnows, alive or dead, make very good bait for pike, perch and eels. Hook them through the lip, like this. Use hook sizes 6-8 for minnow baits.

Try catching minnows in a bottle, like this. Put it in shallow water with bits of bread in it and wait for the minnows to swim in.

Maggots and Casters

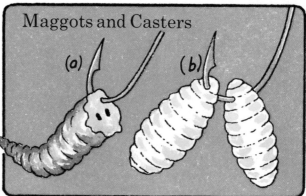

(a) (b)

Maggots – the grubs of flies – are the best kind of freshwater bait. All freshwater fish, except pike, will eat them. Buy them alive from a tackle shop. Hook them like this (a).

A Maggot's Life

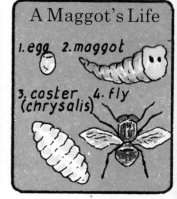

1. egg 2. maggot
3. caster (chrysalis) 4. fly

You can use one or more at a time. Casters (b) – maggots which have turned into chrysalises – also make good bait. Use hook sizes 12 downwards for these baits.

Catching Worms

(a) (b) washing-up liquid and water

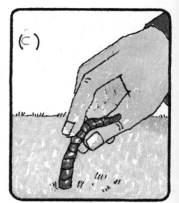

(c)

Lots of freshwater fish like garden worms. Dig them up, or collect them by torchlight on the lawn after dark (a). If you pour water with a

little washing-up liquid over the grass, it helps bring worms out of their holes (b). Pull them out very gently, like this (c). A whole worm is much better than half a worm.

GROUND-BAIT

SOME ANGLERS FIND THAT THEY CATCH MORE FISH IF THEY SCATTER LOTS OF BAIT ROUND THE SPOT WHERE THEY ARE FISHING. YOU CAN DO THIS BY MAKING BALLS OF BAIT, EACH ABOUT THE SIZE OF AN ORANGE, AND THROWING THEM INTO THE WATER WHERE YOU ARE FISHING. AS THE BALLS OF BAIT, CALLED GROUND-BAIT, HIT THE WATER THEY BREAK UP INTO BITS AND SINK TO THE BOTTOM.

IF YOU ARE FISHING IN FLOWING WATER THROW THE GROUND-BAIT JUST UPSTREAM OF THE FISHING SPOT. THEN IT WILL SINK IN THE RIGHT PLACE.

IF YOU ARE FISHING IN STILL WATER THROW THE GROUND-BAIT BALLS STRAIGHT TO THE SPOT YOU ARE GOING TO FISH IN.

Ground-bait for Flowing Water

worms added

When you fish in flowing water, use ground-bait that does not break up too quickly. Soak bits of stale bread in water and squeeze them into balls. Add bits of the hook-bait you are using, such as maggots, bits of worm or cheese.

Still Water Ground-bait

For still water fishing, use ground-bait made out of very small breadcrumbs. They will break up quickly and cloud the water. Roll a bottle over bits of stale bread to make the crumbs. Dampen them and squeeze them into balls.

Making a Wormery

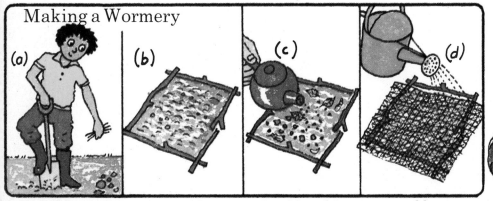

If you make a wormery, you will always have worms for bait. Dig up a patch of earth. Throw away any stones and twigs (a). Then mark the patch with sticks (b).

Mix old tea leaves, vegetable scraps and cut grass in with the soil as often as possible (c). Keep it wet and cover it with sacking (d). Lots of worms will soon wriggle into the wormery.

Hooking Garden Worms

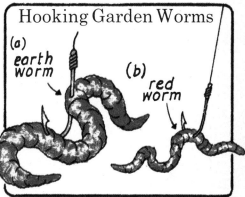

(a) earth worm

(b) red worm

Push the hook twice through a big worm, like this (a). Hook a small one through its middle (b). Use hook sizes 6, 8 or 10 depending on the size of the worm.

Freshwater Float Fishing

A float shows you when a fish bites and keeps the hook at the right depth. Use a float when the water is not very deep. The fishing line you use should be no longer than your rod or it may be difficult to cast.

Use bought floats or the ones you have made. The weights keep the float upright in the water and stop the hook-bait from rising. The amount of weights you need on the line depends on how deep and fast the water is.

First fix the float to the line and put on the weights. Then find out how deep the water is with a plummet to make sure that the hook hangs just above the bottom. Take the plummet off and put bait on the hook.

1 Fixing on the Float

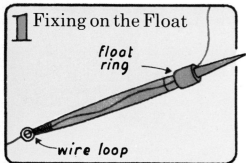

Slide a float ring on to the line about one metre from the end. Push the tip of the float through the ring. Thread the line through the loop on the end of the float.

2

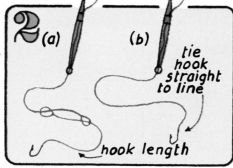

Tie a hook on to the end of the line. Use either a hook length (a) or tie the hook straight on to the line (b). See page 5 for hook lengths and knots.

3

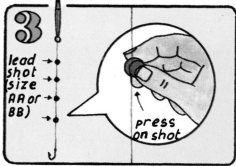

Squeeze enough split shot on to the line to make the float stand upright in the water. Only about 1 cm of the tip should show. This is called cocking the float.

1 Setting the Float

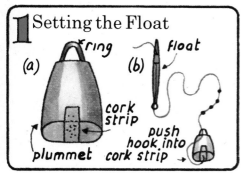

Now use a plummet (a) to find out how deep the water is. Thread the hook and line through the plummet ring and push the hook into the strip of cork (b).

2

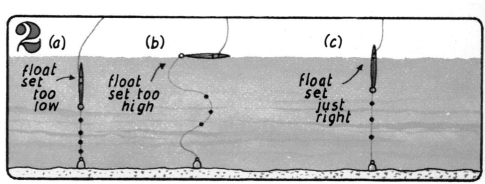

Cast the plummet into the water. If the float goes under, it is set too low (a). If it lies flat on top, it is set too high (b).

Slide the float up or down the line, until just the tip shows above the water when the plummet is on the bottom (c). Take off the plummet and put some bait on to the hook.

Using Floats – Still Water

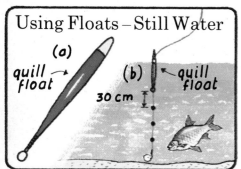

Use a light float such as a quill (a). Squeeze enough shot on to the line to cock the float. Space it out evenly, like this. Then set the float with a plummet (b).

Using Floats – Flowing Water

Use a heavier float, such as an Avon float or peacock quill (a). Group the shot close to the hook so that the bait sinks quickly to the bottom. Cock and set the float.

Once you have set the float, push it up the line another 25 cm. Then the hook-bait will stay on the bottom (b). This sort of tackle is called trotting tackle.

16

Fishing with Trotting Tackle

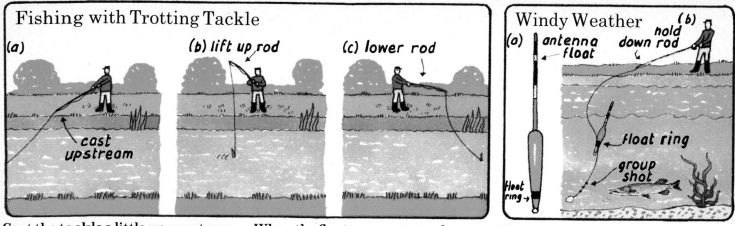

(a)   (b) lift up rod   (c) lower rod

cast upstream

Cast the tackle a little way upstream (a). Keep the line tight. Lift up the end of the rod a bit as the float comes towards you. Point the rod at the float, like this (b).

When the float goes past you, lower the rod a bit. Let it stay downstream for a few seconds (c). If you don't get a bite, reel in the line and cast again.

Windy Weather

(a) antenna float   (b) hold down rod

float ring

group shot

float ring →

Use an antenna float (a). Only thread the line through the float ring. Group the shot as shown and cock the float. Then set it so the bulky part is under the water (b).

1 Laying-on Method

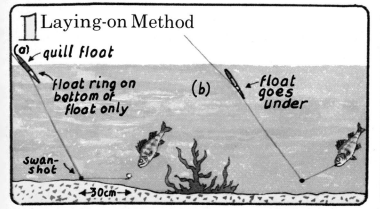

(a) quill float

float ring on bottom of float only

(b)   float goes under

swan-shot

← 30cm →

If you are not getting many bites, try the laying-on (1) or lift (2) methods of fishing. The weight keeps the bait still on the bottom. You can use the laying-on method in both still and flowing water. First cock and set the float.

Then push it up the line another metre. Cast out the line and then tighten it up until only the tip of the float shows (a). When a fish bites, the float will go under the water (b). Use the lift method in still water.

2 Lift Method

(c) float   (d) float lies flat

rubber ring

5cm

Thread the line through a float ring on the bottom of the float only. Cock and set the float so that a swan-shot just rests on the bottom (c). When a fish bites, it lifts the shot off the bottom and the float lies flat on the water (d).

Sinking Bait Quickly

group shot

Sometimes little fish swimming near the top, eat hook-bait before it sinks to where the bigger fish are feeding. Move the shot nearer the hook to make it sink more quickly.

When to Strike

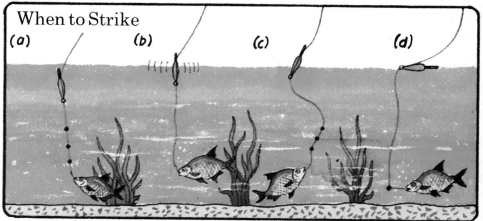

(a)   (b)   (c)   (d)

Striking means lifting up the tip of your rod quickly as soon as a fish takes the bait. As you lift it the line tightens and the hook sticks into the fish's mouth.

Strike if the float goes under the water (a) or wiggles about sideways (b). If it come right up out of the water (c) or lies flat on top (d) strike at once.

Freshwater Leger Fishing

When you fish in deep water, in a strong current or far out from the bank, it is better to use a weight but no float. This is called leger fishing. Leger weights are heavier than the ones you used with a float.

These two pages show you how to make up different kinds of leger tackle for freshwater fishing. The lead weights come in different sizes. Make sure you use one heavy enough to keep the hook-bait in the right spot.

When you have fixed the leger weight on to the line, tie on a hook, put bait on it and cast out. Let the lead settle on the bottom. Then tighten up the line. Hold the rod or use two rod rests while you wait for a bite.

1 Lead Bullet Tackle

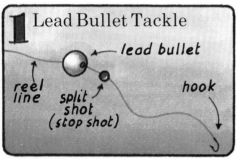

Thread a lead bullet on to the line. Squeeze on a shot, about 45 cm from the hook. The shot stops the bullet from sliding down to the bait. It is called a stop shot.

2

Lead bullet tackle is a good tackle for still or flowing water. It is specially good for catching chub. In rivers, the bullet rolls along the bottom until it gets downstream.

3

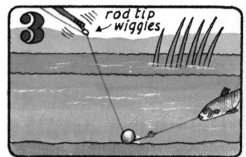

When a fish takes the bait, the line slides through the hole in the lead and the fish does not feel it. Strike when you see the tip of the rod starting to wiggle.

Link Leger Tackle

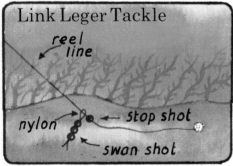

This is a good tackle to use over weedy ground. Loop a bit of nylon line round the reel line. Pinch two or three swan shot on to the nylon line. Then put on a stop shot.

Arlesey Bomb Tackle

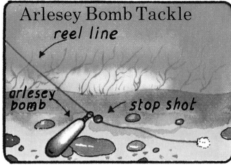

This pear-shaped lead is one of the best leger weights to buy. You can use it in all kinds of water. Thread it on to the reel line and squeeze on a stop shot, like this.

Coffin Lead Tackle

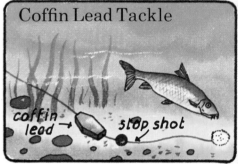

Use a coffin lead over a muddy bottom. The flat shape stops it from sinking into the mud. Thread the lead on to the reel line and then squeeze on a stop shot.

1 Making a Swimfeeder

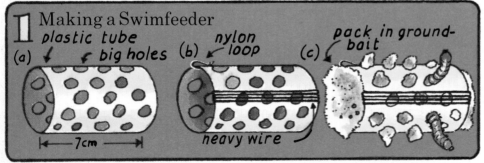

A swimfeeder makes a good leger weight. It also puts ground-bait near the hook-bait in the water. To make one, punch big holes in a small plastic tube with scissors (a).

Wrap some lead wire round one side of the tube to use as a weight. Tie on a small nylon loop (b). Before you start to fish, pack the feeder with bread, bits of worm or some maggots, like this (c).

2

Thread the feeder on to the fishing line and squeeze on a stop shot. When you cast it into the water, the bait comes out of the holes and brings fish to that spot.

ALWAYS KEEP AN EYE ON YOUR ROD TIP OR BITE INDICATOR. IF YOU DOZE OFF OR READ A BOOK YOU MIGHT MISS A BITE OR EVEN LOSE YOUR TACKLE.

Trails

stop shot
(a) long trail
75 cm

(b) short trail
25 cm

The length of line between the stop shot and the hook is called the trail. In flowing water, it should be about 75 cm long (a). In still water, it should be about 25 cm (b).

1 Bite Indicators–Bread Ball

(a) last rod ring
bread paste

(b)
ball pulled against rod

A bite indicator tells you when a fish is biting. The simplest kind is a ball of bread paste. Squeeze it on to the line between the last rod ring and the reel (a).

When a fish takes the hook-bait, it pulls the line tight and the bread ball is pushed up against the rod (b). Strike as soon as you see this happen.

2 –Twig or Silver Paper

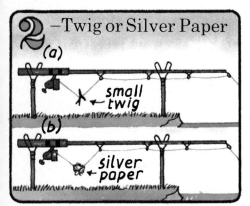

(a) small twig
(b) silver paper

A small twig (a) or a folded piece of silver paper (b) also make good bite indicators. Wait until they are pulled up against the rod before you strike.

3 –Swing-tips

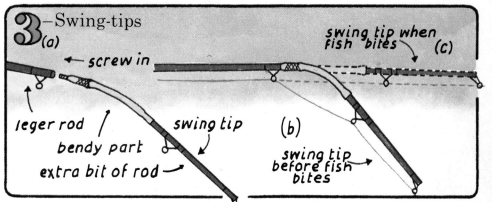

(a) screw in
swing tip when fish bites (c)
leger rod
bendy part
swing tip
extra bit of rod
(b)
swing tip before fish bites

A swing-tip is a bite indicator which screws into the top of a leger fishing rod (a). You can buy one from a fishing tackle shop.

To use it, cast out the leger tackle in the ordinary way. Reel in the line until the swing-tip hangs down (b). As soon as a fish takes the bait, the tip lifts up (c).

River and Stream Fish

These two pages show you where to find fish in flowing water, such as rivers and streams. You might find some of them in still water, such as ponds and lakes, as well. The next two pages show you where to catch fish in still water.

Chub, dace and barbel like fast flowing rivers and streams. Rudd, carp and tench prefer still water. Roach, pike and bream are found in slow running water as well as in still water. Perch, minnows, eels and gudgeon like all kinds of water.

CHUB LURK UNDER OVERHANG TREES AND BUSHE THEY HIDE AMON THE ROOTS OF TREES.

SMALL DACE SWIM ABOUT IN GROUPS IN FAST FLOWING STRETCHES OF WATER. ROACH AND GUDGEON LIVE HERE TOO.

PIKE LURK NEAR REEDBEDS.

SMALL PERCH SWIM EVERYWHERE. BIG ONES STAY CLOSE TO WEEDBEDS OR NEAR BRIDGE SUPPORTS. THEY HUNT SMALL FISH.

Dace love clear, fast flowing water. On warm days they come to the top to catch flies, insects and snails. They will take bait very quickly, so strike fast.

Barbel

Chub

A BARBEL HAS TWO BIG WHISKERS ON EACH SIDE OF ITS LONG SNOUT. IT IS A BIG FISH WITH A STRONG BODY. THE BEST TIME TO CATCH A BARBEL IS AT NIGHT. (AVERAGE LENGTH 45 cm.)

CHUB HAVE BIG HEADS AND LOOK A BIT LIKE TORPEDOES. THEY ARE SOMETIMES MISTAKEN FOR BIG DACE. THEY EAT ANY MOVING BAIT. (AVERAGE LENGTH 30 cm.)

Chub are shy, so be very quiet. Four or five may hide together among the roots of a tree. They feed on frogs, small fish, caterpillars and beetles.

Although gudgeon are very small, they are fun to catch. They like clear, running water and will snap up any small worms you use as bait.

Barbel will fight hard to get away when you hook them. They swim very fast. One of their favourite places is at the bottom of a pool below a weir.

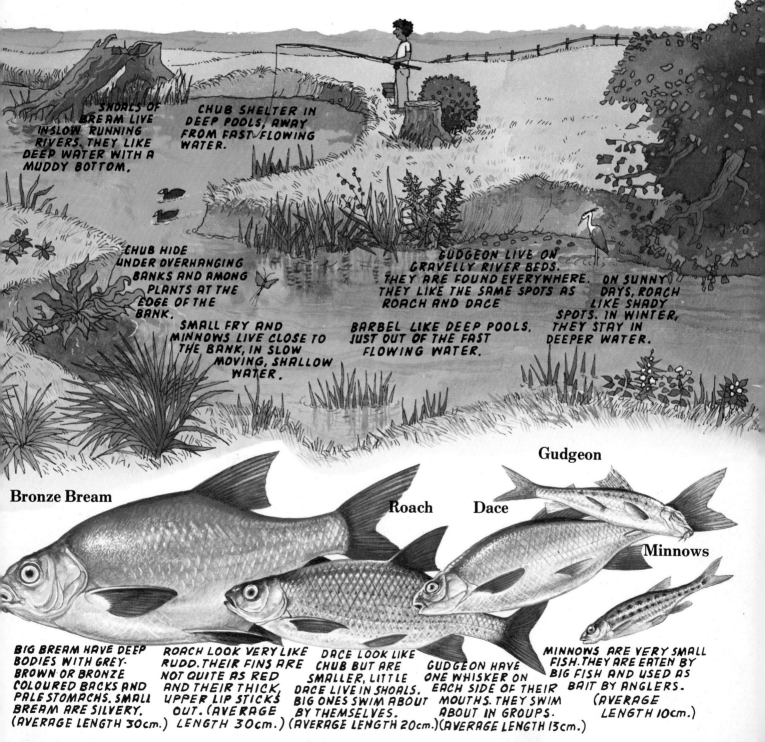

SHOALS OF BREAM LIVE IN SLOW RUNNING RIVERS. THEY LIKE DEEP WATER WITH A MUDDY BOTTOM.

CHUB SHELTER IN DEEP POOLS, AWAY FROM FAST FLOWING WATER.

CHUB HIDE UNDER OVERHANGING BANKS AND AMONG PLANTS AT THE EDGE OF THE BANK.

SMALL FRY AND MINNOWS LIVE CLOSE TO THE BANK, IN SLOW MOVING, SHALLOW WATER.

GUDGEON LIVE ON GRAVELLY RIVER BEDS. THEY ARE FOUND EVERYWHERE. THEY LIKE THE SAME SPOTS AS ROACH AND DACE

BARBEL LIKE DEEP POOLS, JUST OUT OF THE FAST FLOWING WATER.

ON SUNNY DAYS, ROACH LIKE SHADY SPOTS. IN WINTER, THEY STAY IN DEEPER WATER.

Gudgeon

Bronze Bream

Roach　**Dace**

Minnows

BIG BREAM HAVE DEEP BODIES WITH GREY-BROWN OR BRONZE COLOURED BACKS AND PALE STOMACHS. SMALL BREAM ARE SILVERY. (AVERAGE LENGTH 30cm.)

ROACH LOOK VERY LIKE RUDD. THEIR FINS ARE NOT QUITE AS RED AND THEIR THICK, UPPER LIP STICKS OUT. (AVERAGE LENGTH 30cm.)

DACE LOOK LIKE CHUB BUT ARE SMALLER, LITTLE DACE LIVE IN SHOALS. BIG ONES SWIM ABOUT BY THEMSELVES. (AVERAGE LENGTH 20cm.)

GUDGEON HAVE ONE WHISKER ON EACH SIDE OF THEIR MOUTHS. THEY SWIM ABOUT IN GROUPS. (AVERAGE LENGTH 13cm.)

MINNOWS ARE VERY SMALL FISH. THEY ARE EATEN BY BIG FISH AND USED AS BAIT BY ANGLERS. (AVERAGE LENGTH 10cm.)

Pond and Lake Fish

The fish on these two pages are found in still water, such as ponds, lakes; canals and gravel pits. Look at the picture of the lake to find their favourite feeding places. You are most likely to catch them there. Some feed near water plants, overhanging trees and bushes. Others lurk in the reedbeds.

The little pictures round the lake tell you how to catch the fish and show you some of their habits. The big pictures show you what the fish look like and what size they are.

Rudd are always hungry. If you throw bits of crust on the water, they will swim up to eat them. Put a hook through one crust.

MANY FISH, SUCH AS TENCH, BREAM, CARP AND EELS FEED NEAR FALLEN TREES OR BUSHES IN THE WATER.

SHOALS OF BREAM ROAM THE OPEN WATER. THEY FEED AS THEY GO.

PIKE AND PERCH LURK NEAR REEDBEDS AND OTHER HIDING PLACES. THEY GOBBLE UP SMALL FISH AS THEY SWIM BY.

Pike are very greedy. They lie in wait for small or sick fish, snapping them up as they swim by. They are cunning, big fish and very difficult to catch.

Perch nibble at bait before they swallow it. Your float will bob about as they nibble. Don't strike until it goes under the water.

TENCH, BREAM AND CARP LIKE MUDDY BOTTOMED PLACES BELOW LILY PADS AND WATER WEEDS.

Carp

Pike

Eels

EELS SWIM UP RIVERS FROM THE SEA. THEY CAN WRIGGLE OVER WET GRASS TO GET INTO PONDS AND LAKES. (AVERAGE LENGTH 45 cm.)

THE PIKE IS A VERY BIG FISH WITH A LONG GREENISH-YELLOW BODY AND A SNOUT FULL OF SHARP TEETH. IT CAN SWIM VERY FAST. (AVERAGE LENGTH 60 cm.)

CARP ARE BIG AND STRONG. THEY SWIM LAZILY AND LURK IN POOLS. THEY GRIND UP THEIR FOOD WITH FLAT, SHARP TEETH. (AVERAGE LENGTH 45 cm.)

CARP SOMETIMES HIDE IN POOLS BELOW OVERHANGING TREES AND BUSHES.

ROACH AND RUDD LIKE WATER WITH A GRAVELLY BOTTOM. THEY ALSO FEED ON GRUBS AND INSECTS NEAR WATER PLANTS.

MINNOWS AND OTHER LITTLE FISH STAY IN SHALLOW WATER NEAR THE BANK. THEY ARE SAFER FROM BIG FISH HERE.

Watch out for bubbles coming to the top of the water. Tench often make them as they feed (a). They are hard fighters and will thrash about or rush for weedbeds if they are hooked (b).

Bream swim about in big groups called shoals. This makes them easy to catch. They feed in the mud on the bottom of lakes and rivers.

Roach are the most common freshwater fish. They eat grubs and insects off water plants. You can catch them at all levels in the water.

Eels like eating small, dead fish or garden worms. The best time to catch a big eel is in the evening.

Be very quiet and keep out of sight when you fish for carp. Try catching them with crusts of bread.

They are very strong and cunning. Once you hook one it will struggle hard to get away. Hold on tightly to your rod and be prepared to lose a few hooks.

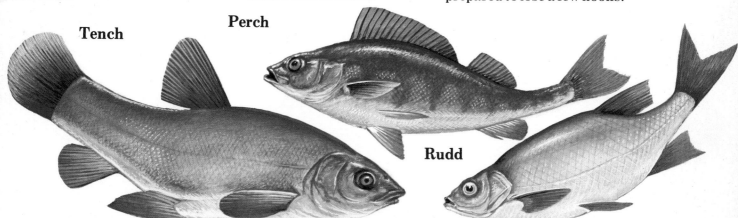

Tench

Perch

Rudd

TENCH ARE QUITE SMALL BUT THEY ARE VERY STRONG. THEY HAVE BRONZE AND DARK GREEN BODIES, RED EYES AND A VERY BROAD TAIL FIN. (AVERAGE LENGTH 25 cm.)

THE PERCH IS A HUNTER WHICH EATS SMALL FISH. IT HAS A BIG SPIKEY MAIN FIN AND A STRIPED BODY. (AVERAGE LENGTH 25 cm.)

RUDD HAVE HUMPED BACKS AND REDDISH FINS. THEIR LOWER LIP STICKS OUT. THIS HELPS THEM TO FEED FROM THE TOP OF THE WATER (AVERAGE LENGTH 25 cm)

Seashore Fishing Baits

All the sea fishing baits you need live on the seashore. The best time to find them is when the tide is out.

Try to keep all your baits alive and fresh. The fish are much more likely to take them like this. Make the drop net on this page to catch prawns for bait.

To use it, tie on bits of fish or worm as bait. Hold the string and let the net sink to the bottom of the pool. Leave it there for a few minutes. Then pull it up quickly.

Making a Drop Net

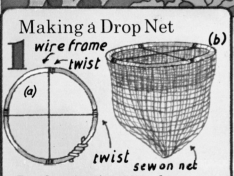

1 *wire frame* *twist* (a) (b) *twist* *sew on net*

Bend some wire, 70 cm long, into a circle. Wind two bits of thin wire on to it, as shown (a). Sew a fine net bag, about 35 cm deep, to the wire frame with string.

2 (a) *knot* (b) *knot* *tie the bait on here* *stone weight*

Tie three long bits of string to the frame and knot them (a). Tie a stone into the bottom of the net. Before you use the net, tie bait to the thin wire (b).

Prawns

(a) (b) *salt water and seaweed* (c)

Prawns are good for catching bass and wrasse. They hide in rock pools under rocks and seaweed. Use your drop net (a) or poke a shrimping net under the rocks to catch them.

Keep prawns alive in a bucket full of seawater and seaweed (b). Hook a prawn through its tail, like this (c).

Crabs

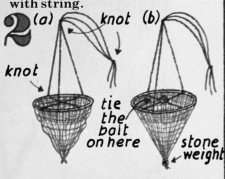

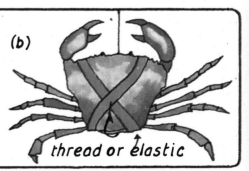

(a) (b) *thread or elastic*

Codling, flounders and bass all like soft-backed crabs. These are crabs that have just out-grown their hard shells. They hide under rocks and seaweed until their new shell hardens (a).

A small crab can be used whole on the hook. Tie it on with an elastic band or some thread, like this (b). Cut big, dead crabs into little pieces.

Lugworms

(a) heap of coiled sand — small dent

(b)

(c) damp sand

(d) plastic box

Lugworms make good bait for most seashore fish. They live on sandy or muddy beaches. At low tide, you will see lots of little curly heaps of sand on the beach.

Close to each heap is a tiny dent. The lugworm lives in a tunnel between the heap and the dent (a). You can dig it out with an ordinary garden fork (b).

Keep lugworms alive in a box filled with damp sand (c). When you use a worm, push the hook through its body, like this (d).

Ragworms

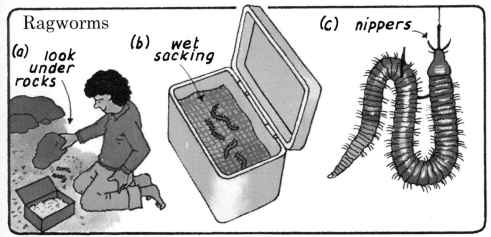

(a) look under rocks

(b) wet sacking

(c) nippers

Ragworms are good bait for bass, pollack and flatfish. They live on muddy and sandy beaches. They also hide under flat rocks and thick seaweed (a).

Keep them alive in a box filled with sacking, rinsed in sea water (b). Be careful of their nippers when you bait up (c). Hold them just behind the head.

Other Baits

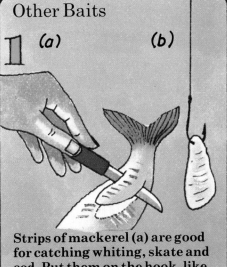

1 (a)   (b)

Strips of mackerel (a) are good for catching whiting, skate and cod. Put them on the hook, like this (b). Use either fresh or frozen mackerel.

Mussels

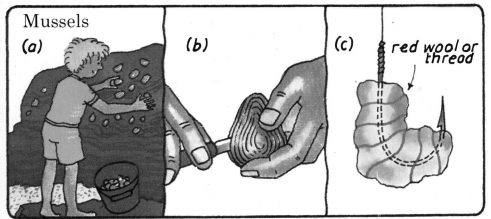

(a)   (b)   (c) red wool or thread

Codling, whiting and flatfish all like mussels. You can pull them off rocks, piers and jetties at low tide (a). Open the shells very carefully with a penknife, like this (b).

Mussels have soft bodies inside their shells. To stop them flying off the hook when you cast, tie them on with red wool or thread (c). Keep them fresh in sea water.

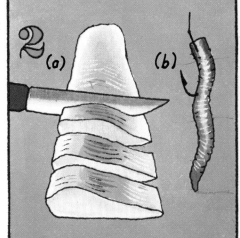

2 (a)   (b)

Herring strips (a) and squid tentacles (b) make good bait for these fish too. They like them even better with a lugworm on the hook as well.

Fishing from the Seashore

Sea Leger Tackle

When you want to cast far out into the water, or fish where the current is strong, use a sea leger tackle or a paternoster tackle.

The lead weight you use must be heavy enough to keep the hook-bait on the bottom. The heavier it is, the further out you will be able to cast the line.

The reel line should have a breaking strain of about 8-10 kg. The hook lengths and paternoster lines about 6-8 kg. Page 5 shows you how to tie all the knots.

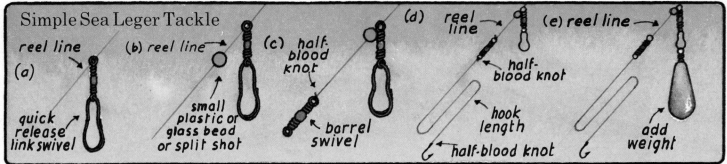

First thread a quick-release spring or link swivel on to the reel line (a). Thread a small, plastic or glass bead just below the swivel (b).

Tie the end of the reel line on to one eye of a barrel swivel (c). Tie a hook length, about 45 cm long, to the other eye of the barrel swivel.

Tie a hook to the end of the hook length (d). Then slip a weight, such as a pear-shaped lead, on to the quick-release swivel (e).

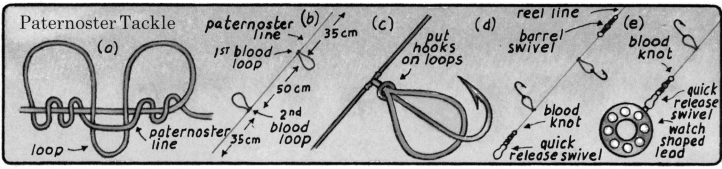

Cut a piece of nylon line, about 1·5 metres long. Tie a blood loop (a) in it. Tie a second loop about 50 cm from the first one (b). This is the paternoster line.

Put a hook on each loop. Do this by threading the loop through the eye and over the hook (c). Pull it tight. Tie one end of the paternoster line to one eye of a barrel swivel.

Tie the end of the reel line to the other eye. Then tie a quick-release swivel to the other end of the paternoster line (d). Slip a lead weight on to the barrel swivel (e).

Lead Weights and Swivels

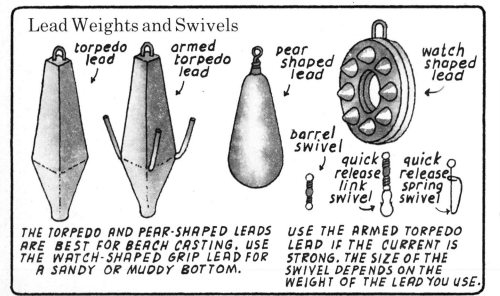

THE TORPEDO AND PEAR-SHAPED LEADS ARE BEST FOR BEACH CASTING. USE THE WATCH-SHAPED GRIP LEAD FOR A SANDY OR MUDDY BOTTOM.

USE THE ARMED TORPEDO LEAD IF THE CURRENT IS STRONG. THE SIZE OF THE SWIVEL DEPENDS ON THE WEIGHT OF THE LEAD YOU USE.

Sea Hooks

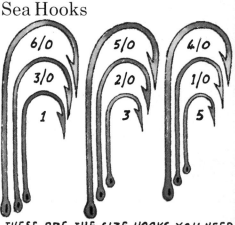

THESE ARE THE SIZE HOOKS YOU NEED FOR SEA FISHING. USE THE LARGER SIZE FOR BIG FISH, SUCH AS COD AND BASS. FOR FLATFISH AND LITTLE FISH, USE THE SMALLER SIZES.

Sea Float Tackle

When the sea is calm and you do not need to cast out too far, use a float instead of a leger or paternoster tackle. It is lighter and easier to cast. Use a reel line with about a 6 kg breaking strain.

Sea floats are usually bigger than freshwater ones. The weights are heavier so that they can cock the float. Lead bullets, spiral or barrel leads are the best kinds of weights to use.

When you float fish in the sea the hook-bait does not have to stay very close to the bottom. It should hang above any rocks and reeds so that the line does not get tangled up.

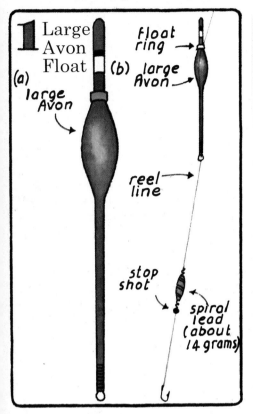

This is a fixed float (a). A fixed float does not slide up and down the fishing line. Put it on the line, like this (b). Put a lead weight and a stop shot half-way between the float and the hook, as shown.

This is another fixed float (a). To put it on the line, take out the wooden peg. Thread the line through the middle of the float and then put the peg back into the float. Fix a weight and a stop shot half-way between the float and the hook (b).

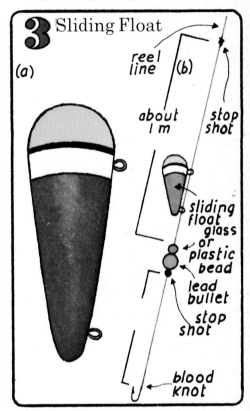

Use a sliding float (a) when the water is deep or you want to fish quite far out. Set up the tackle, like this (b). When it is cast out, the float slides up from the bead to the knot. This stops the line from getting tangled.

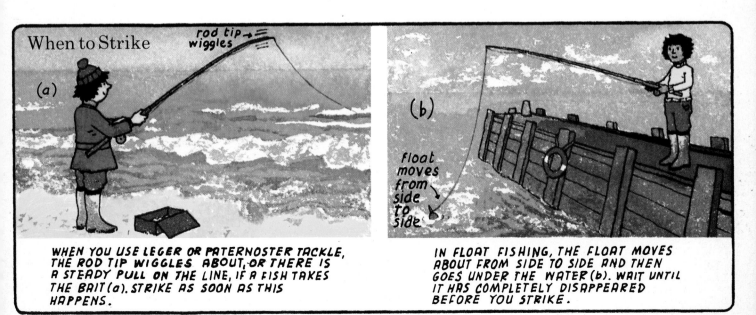

When to Strike

WHEN YOU USE LEGER OR PATERNOSTER TACKLE, THE ROD TIP WIGGLES ABOUT, OR THERE IS A STEADY PULL ON THE LINE, IF A FISH TAKES THE BAIT (a). STRIKE AS SOON AS THIS HAPPENS.

IN FLOAT FISHING, THE FLOAT MOVES ABOUT FROM SIDE TO SIDE AND THEN GOES UNDER THE WATER (b). WAIT UNTIL IT HAS COMPLETELY DISAPPEARED BEFORE YOU STRIKE.

Seashore and Estuary Fish

The best times to go seashore fishing are in the early morning, early evening and the two hours before and after high tide. Lots of different fish swim inshore to feed then.

These are some of the seashore fish you might catch. Look at the four pictures on the right. They show you where the fish live and feed. You are most likely to catch them there.

Flatfish is another name for plaice, flounder and dab. They are called flatfish because of their flat shape. Codling is the name for a young cod.

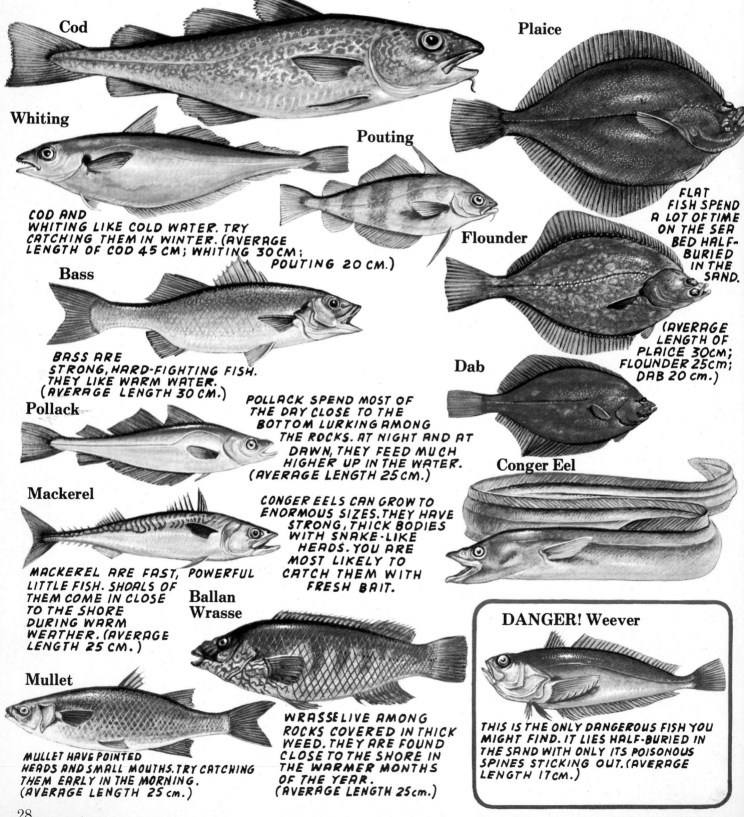

Cod

Plaice

Whiting

Pouting

FLAT FISH SPEND A LOT OF TIME ON THE SEA BED HALF-BURIED IN THE SAND.

COD AND WHITING LIKE COLD WATER. TRY CATCHING THEM IN WINTER. (AVERAGE LENGTH OF COD 45 CM; WHITING 30 CM; POUTING 20 CM.)

Flounder

Bass

BASS ARE STRONG, HARD-FIGHTING FISH. THEY LIKE WARM WATER. (AVERAGE LENGTH 30 CM.)

Dab

(AVERAGE LENGTH OF PLAICE 30cm; FLOUNDER 25cm; DAB 20 CM.)

Pollack

POLLACK SPEND MOST OF THE DAY CLOSE TO THE BOTTOM LURKING AMONG THE ROCKS. AT NIGHT AND AT DAWN, THEY FEED MUCH HIGHER UP IN THE WATER. (AVERAGE LENGTH 25 CM.)

Conger Eel

Mackerel

CONGER EELS CAN GROW TO ENORMOUS SIZES. THEY HAVE STRONG, THICK BODIES WITH SNAKE-LIKE HEADS. YOU ARE MOST LIKELY TO CATCH THEM WITH FRESH BAIT.

MACKEREL ARE FAST, POWERFUL LITTLE FISH. SHOALS OF THEM COME IN CLOSE TO THE SHORE DURING WARM WEATHER. (AVERAGE LENGTH 25 CM.)

Ballan Wrasse

DANGER! Weever

Mullet

MULLET HAVE POINTED HEADS AND SMALL MOUTHS. TRY CATCHING THEM EARLY IN THE MORNING. (AVERAGE LENGTH 25 cm.)

WRASSE LIVE AMONG ROCKS COVERED IN THICK WEED. THEY ARE FOUND CLOSE TO THE SHORE IN THE WARMER MONTHS OF THE YEAR. (AVERAGE LENGTH 25cm.)

THIS IS THE ONLY DANGEROUS FISH YOU MIGHT FIND. IT LIES HALF-BURIED IN THE SAND WITH ONLY ITS POISONOUS SPINES STICKING OUT. (AVERAGE LENGTH 17CM.)

Estuary Fishing

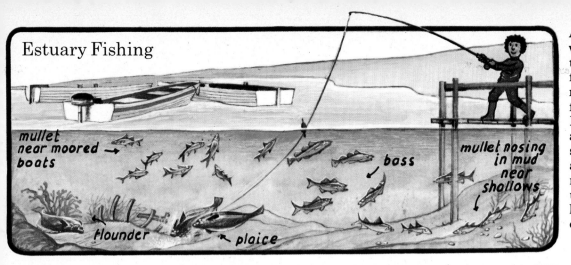

mullet near moored boats

bass

mullet nosing in mud near shallows

flounder

plaice

An estuary–the part where a river flows into the sea – is a very good fishing spot for bass, mullet, plaice, dab, flounder and codling. Mullet like nosing about in the mud in shallow water. They also swim in shoals near moored boats, picking up scraps of food which have been thrown overboard.

You are most likely to catch cod, pouting, whiting and flatfish when you fish from the beach. They swim in close to the shore to find crabs, worms and shellfish. You might also catch bass as they swim into the surf to hunt for crabs and sand-eels. You need to cast your tackle out about 45 metres when you beach fish.

Beach Fishing

open beach

bass in surf

whiting

bass chasing sand eels in the surf

flounder chasing prawn

plaice buried in the sand

cod eating hermit crab

Rock Fishing

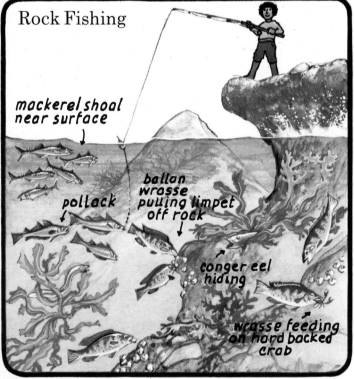

mackerel shoal near surface

pollack

ballan wrasse pulling limpet off rock

conger eel hiding

wrasse feeding on hard backed crab

Find a rocky platform over the sea, when you go rock fishing. You will be able to see far out and there will be deep water within easy reach. Wrasse, mackerel, pollack and conger eels all feed in rocky bays. Be careful of a conger. It is very strong and has a mouth full of sharp teeth.

Pier Fishing

pouting

whiting

cod

conger eel in hiding place

flounder buried

When you fish from a pier or jetty, drop your tackle straight down beside its supports. Flatfish, cod, whiting and pouting stay close to them, searching for food hidden in the seaweed. Conger eels hide between rocks and at the bottom of the pier legs among thick seaweed.

Do's and Don'ts

Before you go fishing, check the weather forecast. It is not much fun getting caught in a gale or thunder storm.

Always tell someone where you are going and what time you think you will be home. Take something to eat and drink if you will be away all day.

It is a good idea to go fishing with a friend. Then there is always someone about to help if anything goes wrong.

Permits and Licences

Fishing from the seashore is free for everyone. Fishing in freshwater is usually private and may cost you a little. Before you start to fish find out if you need a rod licence or fishing permit. You will probably need both. The local tackle dealer or fishing club will be able to sell them to you or tell you where to get them.

In most places you are not allowed to fish during some months of the year. It depends on what part of the country you are in and what kind of fish you want to catch. Ask the tackle dealer about this too.

Find out which fish you have to put back into the water and which ones you can keep.

What to Wear

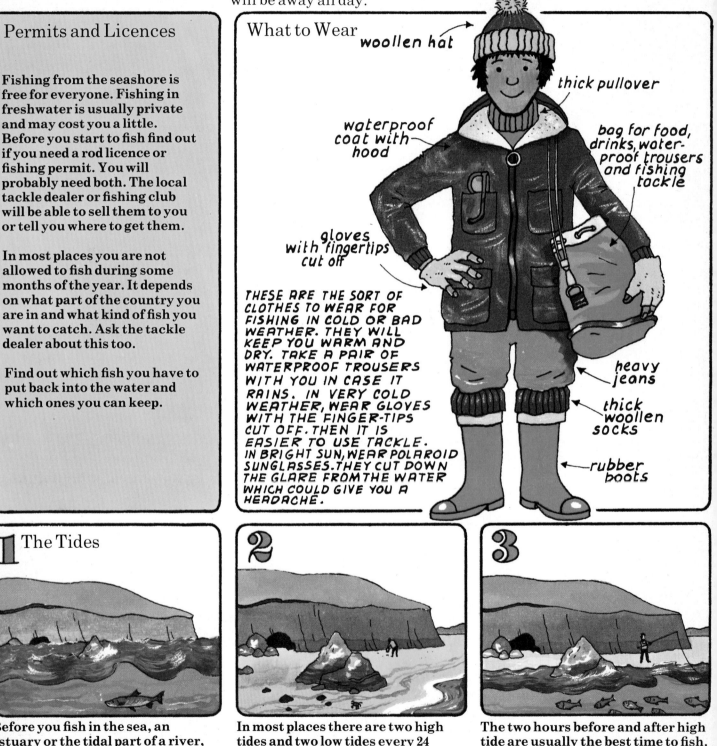

woollen hat

thick pullover

waterproof coat with hood

bag for food, drinks, waterproof trousers and fishing tackle

gloves with fingertips cut off

heavy jeans

thick woollen socks

rubber boots

THESE ARE THE SORT OF CLOTHES TO WEAR FOR FISHING IN COLD OR BAD WEATHER. THEY WILL KEEP YOU WARM AND DRY. TAKE A PAIR OF WATERPROOF TROUSERS WITH YOU IN CASE IT RAINS. IN VERY COLD WEATHER, WEAR GLOVES WITH THE FINGER-TIPS CUT OFF. THEN IT IS EASIER TO USE TACKLE. IN BRIGHT SUN, WEAR POLAROID SUNGLASSES. THEY CUT DOWN THE GLARE FROM THE WATER WHICH COULD GIVE YOU A HEADACHE.

1 The Tides

Before you fish in the sea, an estuary or the tidal part of a river, find out the times of high and low tide. Get a tide table from a fishing shop or club.

2

In most places there are two high tides and two low tides every 24 hours. The times change slightly every day. Make sure you do not get cut off by an incoming tide.

3

The two hours before and after high tide are usually the best time to fish. This is when the fish come near the shore to feed. Low tide is the best time to collect bait.

The Country Code

1 Don't

It is very important to look after fishing places. This picture shows you what might happen if you don't.

Never leave rubbish about or break down trees or bushes. Don't throw away bits of nylon line or any old hooks.

They can easily kill or hurt birds and little animals. Close gates behind you and try not to damage lake or river banks.

2 Do

These are some of the things you should do. Remember to put fish back in the water if you are not going to keep them.

Don't just throw them back. Put them in your landing net and lower them gently into the water.

Move about very quietly so you don't disturb any other anglers nearby. Always read your fishing permit carefully and follow all the rules.

Angling Clubs

If you join an angling club, you will get plenty of chances for good fishing. It costs very little to become a member.

Some clubs own stretches of water. They arrange fishing and matches for their members. Beginners get help and lots of fishing tips.

Ask at a tackle shop or local library for the names and addresses of nearby clubs. Ring up the Secretary or just go along.

Anglers' Words

Baiting up – putting bait on the hook before you cast your fishing line into the water.

Breaking strain – the weight a fishing line can take without breaking. The thicker the line, the more weight it can take.

Casting – swinging the rod and line to put the bait into the water in the right place.

Cocking the float – making the float stand upright in the water by putting weights below it on the line.

Downstream – the part of a river or stream where the water is flowing away from you.

Fixed spool reel – a reel with a metal arm which winds line on to the spool.

Ground-bait – balls of bait made of bread, maggots or worms which you throw into the water near your fishing spot to attract the fish.

Hook-bait – bait which you put on the hook to make the fish bite.

Hook length – a piece of nylon line with a hook on the end which is joined to the reel line.

Reel line – the fishing line which you wind on to your reel.

Setting the drag – making sure the nut on the front of the reel is loose enough to let the line run out without breaking when you hook a big fish.

Setting the float – sliding the float up or down the line so that the hook-bait hangs below it at the right depth.

Split shot – small lead balls which you squeeze on to the line to cock the float or anchor leger tackle.

Stop shot – a split shot which you put on the line to stop a leger weight from sliding down to the hook.

Striking – quickly lifting up the tip of your rod when the fish bites so that the hook sticks in the fish's mouth.

Swim – the area of water you cast into.

Tackle – the name for all the gear you use to fish with.

Trail – the length of line between the weight and the hook in leger fishing.

Upstream – the part of a river or stream where the water is flowing towards you.

Index